JF GOODMAN
Goodman, Chasitie.
Could I really be president?

Could I Really Be President?

Chasitie Sharron Goodman

ISBN 978-1-68222-952-1

DEDICATION

To Mary Amanda Goodman, my loving grandmother who watches over me from the Spirit's Realm, and who watched a very historic election from the Heavens.

&

To Barack Obama, the first Black President of the United States.

ACKNOWLEDGMENTS

Lee and Doretta Goodman, eternal lovebirds and the GREATEST parents a child could ask for. Your undying support, wisdom and love have been vital to me. Thank you for life.

Lee Goodman Jr., my best friend, and brother, thank you for your encouragement, amazing conversations, and just your presence. The world is waiting for you.

Blue Rasberry Wind, a Master Teacher, and my patient mentor. Thank you for all of your gracious assistance, wisdom, and for keeping me mindful, I am ever grateful.

Dr. William Hardy, my favorite teacher, and a major inspiration, may you rest in paradise.

To all my students, the past, present, and future; you all inspire me, keep me grounded in love, and move me beyond words.

&

The Spirit's Realm, my Spirit Guides, the Seen and the Unseen who assist me in my graceful arrival in every moment. Thank you.

My name is Isaiah; I am eight years old. For the first time, I stayed home from school today. I never get to do that! My grandma convinced my parents that it was okay. I couldn't believe it! My mom and dad, my grandparents, and all my aunts, uncles, and cousins came to my house. My grandma told me that today was a very, very, special occasion.

All the ladies in my family got up extra early to make a big breakfast for our family. My mom and aunts played loud music, danced around, and cooked with joy. I helped them to set the scrumptious breakfast on the table. My grandma says scrumptious; that means that it is sooooo good! My family and I pass food, laugh, and talk like we do when something big is going to happen!

After we had finished eating, my aunt Tia stood to make sure that everyone had their jobs for the day. All the adults were to take turns watching the youngest of us. There were children under 18, so we were to stay together, listen, and be on our best behavior. My family was on their way to vote for the next president of the United States.

My grandpa said that this was a very special day, one that he never thought he would see. Black people in this country have fought a long time to receive fair treatment. Grandpa said that we were once slaves in this country and that we were not allowed in certain places. We were thought of as monsters because we were Black.

Grandma said that because our skin was not White, we were treated like monsters too. Black people were killed without reason, thrown in jails for no reason, and were not allowed to do the same things as White people. Many brave people fought for equal treatment of Blacks and Whites, people of all colors and ages.

"Some people thought this day would never come, but here we are." Daddy replied.

My mother was thoughtful, and added that we should be proud on this day and walk with our heads held high because we were all going to help put someone that looks like us, someone with beautiful melanated skin like ours, into the White House. "For the first time in American history," my mom said, "a Black man could be the most powerful leader of the most powerful country in the world."

Excitedly, I ran upstairs to get dressed. The whole family got all dressed up too. We had to pile into three cars! We drove up to a school; daddy said that this is where the adults were going to vote. We all got into a line.

Many, many, people gathered to vote! There were all colors of people, people of all sizes, and some people that spoke different languages. Some laughed loudly, and some Black people sang songs. There were some young people there, like my cousins and I, and some Black people were very old and had to be helped to walk and to sit.

My grandfather's time finally came to vote. My mom snapped a picture of him and me with her cellular phone before he voted. He showed the poll helpers his identification. One of the poll helpers showed him to a voting booth. When my grandfather went in, he was hidden behind a large cloth. Once my grandfather voted, the poll helper gave him a t-shirt. My grandpa whispered something to the poll helper, and they both smiled.

When my grandpa came out of the voting room my family cheered! He bent down and helped me put on the shirt. It said, "I voted". "I just voted for an African-American to hold the highest office in the land." he said. "Maybe someday, your momma and daddy will vote for you!" I thought about that for a long, long, time. Could I really be president?

It took a long time, but finally all the adults in my family had voted, and we all had, "I voted" t-shirts. My family beamed with pride. Someone volunteered to take a picture of us all with my mom's cell phone.

That night, my whole family stayed up late to watch
the election on television. My family seemed to be kind of
nervous.

Suddenly, my family started to dance, and high five. Then finally, the newscaster announced the winner of the election; my cousins and I squealed and jumped up and down! My dad was jumping up and down with us. My mom and my aunts cheered and screamed!

My grandparents were crying. "I can't believe it." my
grandpa said, "It happened, we are going to have a Black
president! The highest office in the land! I can't believe
it!" "He stands in protection too." my grandma said. "All
of the ancestors, angels, and the spirits stand around
him! Look at him, walking out there not scared of
nothing!"

I pondered what that meant, to truly not be scared of "nothing". "I am not scared of nothing either!" I thought. "I am not scared of nothing either!"

"I have lived to see 85 years," my grandma said, "and good gracious, I've seen Black people do many awesome things, captivate the nation, invent things, make beautiful art, and survive many difficult situations, but I never thought I'd see a Black man be president!"

"Me either momma," my daddy said, "me either." My family all hummed in agreement.

That night, I stayed awake in my bed for a long time and thought about everything that had happened. I thought about by grandma and grandpa. I thought about all of the stories that they told me about what it meant to be a Black person. I thought about how amazing it was not to have limits.

I snuck out of my bed and tipped to where my grandparents were. They were not sleeping yet. They were talking quietly. They looked up at me. "What are you doing?" they said in unison. They do that sometimes. My grandma says that that's what married couples do. "I can't sleep; I keep thinking about everything!" I said.

I looked at my grandma. "Thank you for not making me go to school today. I am not old enough to vote yet, but I will always remember today because my family helped change the world." My grandmother had tears rolling down her face. "We did, didn't we? Now, get some rest my love." We gave each other another tight hug, and I went back to bed.

The next morning, my family woke up in a rush, excitedly talking about our new president and all the stories that my grandparents told. I had to get ready for school. After I took a bath and brushed my teeth; I stood up very straight and tried to look official and important as I looked in the mirror.

"The President of the United States looks like me," I thought. "Wow, He looks like me! I could win an election one day. Maybe I'll be president when he gets done."

"Isaiah!" my mother called.

"I will never forget that day," I thought.

"Isaiah!" my mom called again.

I glanced in the mirror one last time, "Coming!" I said.

ABOUT THE AUTHOR

Chasitie Sharron Goodman is a writer, and an educator. She is a lover of family and she seeks to empower children and their families with positivity, love, and diverse perspectives.